"Kids know nothing about racism.
They're taught that by adults."

—Ruby Bridges

For my daughter, KSBC

For B

For our antiracist heroes everywhere!

Bala Kids
An imprint of Shambhala Publications, Inc.
2129 13th Street
Boulder, Colorado 80302
www.shambhala.com

Cover art: Letícia Moreno
Design: Kara Plikaitis

9 8 7 6 5 4 3 2 1

First Edition
Printed in Malaysia

Shambhala Publications makes every effort to print on acid-free, recycled paper.
Bala Kids is distributed worldwide by Penguin Random House, Inc., and its subsidiaries.

Library of Congress Cataloging-in-Publication Data
Names: Bacon, Jennifer Nicole, author. | Moreno, Letícia (Illustrator), illustrator.
Title: I am an antiracist superhero!: with activities to help you be one too! / Jennifer Nicole Bacon; illustrated by Letícia Moreno.
Description: First edition. | Boulder, Colorado: Bala Kids, [2023]
Identifiers: LCCN 2022013244 | ISBN 9781645470984 (hardback)
Subjects: LCSH: Anti-racism—United States—Juvenile literature. | Racial Justice—United States—Juvenile literature. | Interpersonal relations in children—United States—Juvenile literature. | Compassion in children—United States—Juvenile literature. | United States—Race relations—Juvenile literature.
Classification: LCC E184.A1 B223 2023 | DDC 305.800973—dc23/eng/20220812
LC record available at https://lccn.loc.gov/2022013244

I AM an ANTIRACIST SUPERHERO

Jennifer Nicole Bacon

bala kids

Illustrated by Letícia Moreno

"No Justice! No Peace!"

Malik was mesmerized! He saw the signs and heard the chant as protestors marched down the street.

"What's happening?" Malik asked.

Mommy and Daddy looked at each other with concern. Mommy answered, "They are marching in protest because of what happened to George Floyd."

"Who is George Floyd?" Malik asked.

"George Floyd was a Black man who was killed by the police because of the color of his skin." Daddy said seriously. "Being mean or hurting someone because of the color of their skin is racism."

"That's not fair,"
Malik declared.

"And it feels
scary too."

"Do you know what helps me when I feel scared?" Mommy asked, hugging Malik.

"I think of people who I can look up to. People who I think are brave. It makes me feel stronger."

"Real-life heroes are people who speak out against injustice when they see it. People like Rosa Parks, James Baldwin, Ruby Bridges, and Wynta-Amor Rogers," said Daddy.

Rosa Parks

James Baldwin

Rosa Parks was a civil rights activist. She refused to give up her seat on a bus to a white man during segregation. This started the bus boycott that ended bus segregation.

James Baldwin was a writer and civil rights activist. He wrote about racism to change it and create equality.

Ruby Bridges

Wynta-Amor Rogers

Ruby Bridges was the first African American child to desegregate white schools in the South. She was six years old! Because of her, and other brave children and adults like her, all children were able to go to school together in the United States.

Wynta-Amor Rogers was seven years old when she marched against racism at the George Floyd protests. She's an antiracist, which means she's against racism.

"Wynta-Amor is in first grade, just like you. You could even say she's a superhero—an antiracist superhero!" said Daddy.

"I can be a hero too!" Malik declared.

"Yes, you can, honey!" Mommy cheered.

"One of the first things that you can do is remember to Look, Listen, Feel, and then Act," Daddy said.

"When following these four steps, you, too, can make a difference. Sometimes you might get scared—even heroes get scared sometimes," Mommy added.

"But remember, you can always count on us," she said. "We're here to love and protect you."

Malik stood up, excited. "Now I can share what I learned about Look, Listen, Feel, and Act with my friends!"

"My name is Malik, and I am an antiracist superhero!"

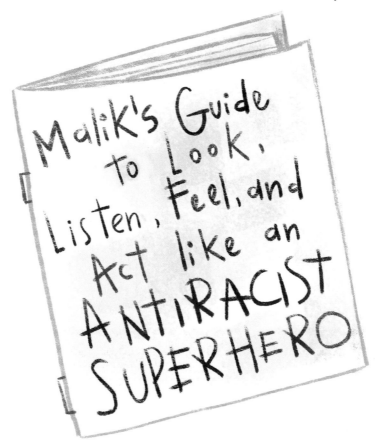

What are your Superpowers?

My friends and I don't all look alike.
But we all have something in common.

We Look, Listen, Feel, and Act to help make things fair for everyone.

Look like a SUPERHERO

First, antiracist superheroes use their senses to look for ways to make their schools, neighborhoods, and the world a better place.

Jamal: "I look to see if someone is left out on the playground."

Adam: "I look to see if someone is being made fun of."

Annie: "I look to see if someone doesn't have something to play with."

LISTEN like a SUPERHERO

Next, antiracist superheroes recognize that listening is one of the greatest superpowers of all because it shows kindness.

Keisha: "I listen when someone shares their feelings."

Mohammad: "I listen when my friends say they need help."

Camille: "I listen by looking at my friend when she is talking, then repeat what she said to check that I understand."

FEEL like a SUPERHERO

And then antiracist superheroes do something really cool: You stop and take a deep breath, making sure to notice your feelings. Whether you feel good or bad, it is brave to feel all your feelings.

Carlos: "I feel proud when I treat everyone fairly."

Felicia: "I feel sorry when I say something mean."

Haru: "I feel angry when I hear someone say hurtful things about others."

ACT like a SUPER HERO

Once you've looked, listened, and felt, you are ready to act!
Everyone can take action to make the world a fairer place.

Malik: "I act by including someone who is being left out."

Aleta: "I act by saying kind words when someone is scared."

Ming: "I act by letting my parents know when I see something that is not fair."

Our real superpowers are kindness, justice, love, and support. *We are the Antiracist Superheroes!*

Here are more ways you can Look, Listen, Feel, and Act like an Antiracist Superhero!

LOOK Like A SUPERHERO
ACTIVITY

Reflection

Have you ever noticed anyone being left out? What does it look like when someone is being made fun of? Have you ever been left out or made fun of?

Vision Board

1. Use a large poster board and your favorite art supplies, such as markers, paints, collage materials like magazine pictures and glitter, and anything else you like.

2. Close your eyes and picture a world of peace, fairness, and togetherness. What does it look like to you? What does it look like for everyone to be included?

3. Create a picture of that world on your poster board. You can draw, paint, sketch, or create a collage of what you see.

Reflection

How can you show compassion, kindness, and understanding while listening to others? Are there times when you felt you weren't listened to? When someone needs help or wants to share their feelings, what is the best way to show you are listening to them?

Listen with Your Senses

1. Find a partner to do this activity with you.

2. First, sit in a comfortable position and take a moment to be still. Say to yourself, "I am present." Take a deep breath in and a deep breath out. Repeat this three times.

3. Then take turns sharing your thoughts and feelings. Think about questions like:

   - *What are you feeling now?*
   - *What makes you feel happy?*
   - *What makes you feel angry?*
   - *What makes you feel sad?*
   - *Who do you talk to or what do you do to feel better?*

4. After you share, ask your partner what they heard you say. Do they have any questions you can answer?

5. Then switch roles. As your partner speaks, use your listening superpowers. How can you let your partner know that you are listening?

   - *Do you look at them while they're speaking?*
   - *Do you nod and listen quietly?*
   - *Do you tell them what you heard and ask questions after they are finished talking?*

Feel Like Activity A Superhero

Reflection

What makes you feel happy and included? What are the good feelings that dry your tears and feel like the warmest hug? What makes you feel brave? What about when you feel bad—what makes you sad or angry? Think about your different feelings and how you can share them.

Feeling Jars

1. Being able to share with someone how you're feeling is a good way to start a conversation. These feeling jars can help get you started! To make your feeling jars, gather:

   - five or more small plastic jars
   - strips of paper
   - tape
   - a pen
   - several different colors of pom-poms or pieces of paper

2. Get help from an adult to write on the strips of paper what kind of feelings you feel, and tape each one to a separate jar. Maybe you want to make an angry jar, a happy jar, a frustrated jar, a confused jar, a sad jar, or even a silly jar.

3. Pick your favorite color of pom-poms or paper to represent your feelings. What are you feeling now? Put your pom-pom into the jar that reflects or shows your feelings. If you decide to, you can share your feeling jars with a trusted adult or friend.

4. Feelings can change. If you put your pom-pom in your angry jar and then start to feel better, you can take the pom-pom out of the angry jar and put it into the happy jar. You can also have mixed feelings, and you might put pom-poms in both the mad and the frustrated jars.

Act Like a Superhero Activity

Reflection

Everyone has something they can offer to make the world a more just place. These are your superpowers! What is one thing you would like to do to make your house, classroom, park or playground, or neighborhood a better place? How can you team up with other superheroes and take action?

What Are Your Superpowers?

1. Write out or say a list of your superpowers, such as:

   - good listening

   - sharing

   - making people laugh

   - speaking up for others

2. Draw or paint a picture of your superpowers. What can you do with your superpowers?

3. Use your superpowers to help people!

   - If you are great at making people laugh, create a funny card for someone who needs a smile.

   - If your superpower is speaking up for others, ask your parent or teacher for help with writing a letter about a rule that you would like to see changed.

   - If your superpower is good listening, you can visit a home for the elderly to spend time with the residents.

GLOSSARY

"But what does that *mean*?" Antiracism is a difficult subject to grasp for adults, let alone children! This glossary is meant as a resource for parents, caregivers, and teachers who, as they read along with children and talk about the book, may run into words or concepts that have more abstract meanings. The definitions are child-friendly and meant as a starting point for further discussions.

ACTIVISM is taking action to help others and make the world a better place. *Activists* are people who do this work.

ANTIRACISM is an idea as well as the act of being against *racism*, which means beliefs and behaviors that treat Black people and other people of color unfairly. *Antiracists* are people who speak out against unfairness and promote equality for all people.

BLACK LIVES MATTER is a movement—a group of people working together—that started in 2013 to support justice and fair treatment of Black people.

BOYCOTT means not to use, buy, or take part in something because it is unfair to others. For example, during the bus boycott in 1955, people did not ride the buses because they made Black people sit separately from white people.

CIVIL RIGHTS are personal rights that make sure everyone is equal, which means they do not leave out anyone based on race, gender, disabilities, or other qualities.

COMPASSION is when you show concern or understanding when someone is hurt. When someone acts compassionately, they help to make things better.

DESEGREGATION is the end of *segregation*, which means separating people because of the color of their skin.

DISCRIMINATION is any unfair treatment of other people, especially based on race, gender, ability, and age.

DIVERSITY means including people of all backgrounds, races, abilities, and other qualities.

EQUITY means making sure that everyone has what they need. An equitable society is one where all people have what they need to succeed.

JUSTICE is fairness. Supporting justice means speaking up for equal and fair treatment for all people.

RACE is an idea that people are divided into separate groups based on the color of their skin and other differences that you can see.